# WELCOME TO
# PASSPORT TO READING
## A beginning reader's ticket to a brand-new world!

Every book in this program is designed to build read-along and read-alone skills, level by level, through engaging and enriching stories. As the reader turns each page, he or she will become more confident with new vocabulary, sight words, and comprehension.

These PASSPORT TO READING levels will help you choose the perfect book for every reader.

### READING TOGETHER
Read short words in simple sentence structures together to begin a reader's journey.

### READING OUT LOUD
Encourage developing readers to sound out words in more complex stories with simple vocabulary.

### READING INDEPENDENTLY
Newly independent readers gain confidence reading more complex sentences with higher word counts.

### READY TO READ MORE
Readers prepare for chapter books with fewer illustrations and longer paragraphs.

This book features sight words from the educator-supported Dolch Sight Word List. Readers will become more familiar with these commonly used vocabulary words, increasing reading speed and fluency.

For more information, please visit www.passporttoreadingbooks.com, where each reader can add stamps to a personalized passport while traveling through story after story!

*Enjoy the journey!*

**MARVEL**

Little, Brown and Company

Hachette Book Group
237 Park Avenue, New York, NY 10017
Visit our website at www.lb-kids.com

LB kids is an imprint of Little, Brown and Company. The LB kids name and logo
are trademarks of Hachette Book Group, Inc.

The publisher is not responsible for websites (or their content)
that are not owned by the publisher.

First Edition: September 2011

ISBN 978-0-316-17630-9

Library of Congress Control Number: 2011926079

10 9 8 7 6 5 4 3 2 1

CW

Printed in the United States of America

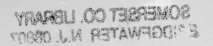

# THE TROUBLE WITH THOR

by Lucy Rosen
illustrated by Dario Brizuela
inks by Andres Ponce

LITTLE, BROWN & COMPANY
**LB kids**

**Attention, Super Hero Squad fans! Look for these items when you read this book. Can you spot them all?**

**SLIDE**

**POWER LINES**

**HAMMER**

**LIGHTNING BOLT**

Thor wakes up one day
with a knot in his stomach.
"I have a bad feeling about today,"
he says with a shiver.

Thor tries to ignore his nerves.
He has to help the other Squaddies
build a new park in Super Hero City.
He needs to leave or he will be late.

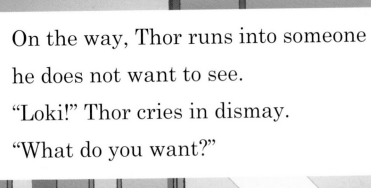

On the way, Thor runs into someone he does not want to see.

"Loki!" Thor cries in dismay.

"What do you want?"

"Can't a villain visit
his favorite half brother?"
Loki asks with a smirk.

"Never! Now beat it!" yells Thor.

"Fine," says Loki. "I will go.

But you know I am right!"

Loki's words scare Thor.

The knot in his stomach feels bigger.

Thor finally arrives at the park.

"There you are!" says Silver Surfer.

"We have a lot to do today.

Can you put this slide together?"

"No problem," says Thor.

He lifts his hammer and swings.

He swings too hard. BOOM!

The hammer smashes the slide!

"Are you okay?" asks Silver Surfer.

"I am fine," says Thor.

"I will fix that later.

What else can I do?"

"We need to fill the pool,"

says Dr. Strange.

"Can you make it rain just a little?"

Thor nods. That is easy.
He zaps the sky with his hammer
to make a small rain shower.
But the storm gets out of control.

It turns into a huge hailstorm!
Wind knocks over the power lines.
The Super Heroes run for cover!

"I am sorry!" yells Thor.
Thor stops the storm.
The park is in ruins.
He feels terrible.

Thor does not know what to do.
Should he leave Super Hero City?
Should he go live in Villainville?

Back at Squad headquarters,
Thor hears an alarm.

"It's Magneto and Doc Ock!"
yells General Ross.

"They are attacking! We need you!"

Thor reaches the fight
as Magneto knocks Falcon down.
Doc Ock pins Iceman
with his long mechanical arms.

Things look bad
for the Super Hero Squad!

Thor's stomach tightens.

He worries he will mess up again,

but he has to try to help his friends!

He throws a lightning bolt at Doc Ock.

It shocks the villain's metal arms.

Doc Ock lets go of Iceman.

Thor makes rain, which rusts Doc Ock.

The villain cannot move his metal arms!

Magneto uses his magnetic force to drag Doc Ock behind him. He runs off, yelling to Thor, "You will never catch me!"

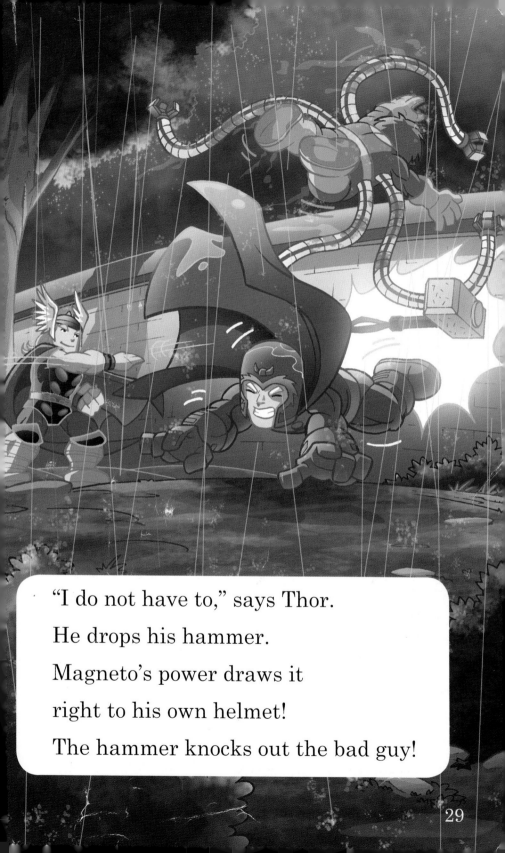

"I do not have to," says Thor.

He drops his hammer.

Magneto's power draws it

right to his own helmet!

The hammer knocks out the bad guy!

"Even Super Heroes have bad days," says General Ross. "It did not stop you when we needed you most."

Thor smiles.

The knot in his stomach goes away.

He knows he is right where he belongs.